CW00881544

The PEOPLE ZOO

by Octavia Lindlahr

Illustrations by Mike Motz

WELCOME
TO THE
PEOPLE ZOO

This book is dedicated
to my son, Maximus, my grandson, Ollin,
and all the children in the world whom I hope learn
at an early age that we share our planet with animals.
We are not superior to them.
They are our furry, scaled, winged and feathered,
two, four (and more) legged brothers and sisters
who are, in most cases, smarter, more loving,
and more compassionate than we humans are.
We can learn from the animals.

Once upon a time, but not a long time from now,
on this planet that we call Earth,
friends from a distant land were watching us.
They were curious.

And they were friendly.
They lived on their own planet, but they liked
to come to Earth to see how human people lived.
Everything we did was different from
how they did it on their own planet.

They found it interesting to see how we looked,
how we worked, how we played,
how we slept, and what we ate.

Everything about us was fascinating to them. They wanted to be our friends and learn more about us. They wanted to teach their children about human people.

So, they landed their super cool spaceship
and started making friends.

They made friends at the bank.

They made friends at the hospitals.

They made friends at the Senior Citizen
and Nursing Homes.

They even made friends with people
from different countries.

They made friends with people
who live in the forests...

...and even people in the ocean!

Before you knew it, more and more of the "friends from another planet" came to live on Earth with us.

They liked Earth. It was different than their planet. It was interesting, and they wanted to learn more. One day the "friends from another planet" got together and decided that the best way to learn about us humans was to start a "People Zoo."

WELCOME TO THE PEOPLE ZOO

They would be able to watch us, observe us, and even teach the children "from another planet" about us. It would be "educational" and all the "friends from another planet" would come to see the people. It would be a great "learning experience."

So, the "friends from another planet"
built a beautiful structure. It was big and clean,
but not very spacious for all the people.
It had very nice "friends from another planet"
to run it and work there to help
care for all the people.

The next step was to gather people from different places so the "friends from another planet" could fill the People Zoo with many types of different people from all over the world. This would be the best way to learn about people, they thought.

They made sure to get people from different places like India.

Africa.

Japan.

Russia.

Alaska.

Jamaica.

Nepal.

And even New York City...

... and Los Angeles!

Some of the people they took from
these places were children, and it made them
sad to leave their families.

The "friends from another planet" were convinced that all the people going to the People Zoo would be happy because they would be well taken care of.

They would have food, a place to sleep, and lots of attention from the "friends from another planet."

However, it did not take long before the people in the People Zoo were unhappy. They missed their families. They missed their homes and their friends.

Some were not used to the climate
in their new habitats.

Some did not like the food, and they all missed playing in their own space, with their own toys.

Some people became very sad and depressed.
It was true, they were being fed, and the "friends
from another planet" took very good care of them,
but it wasn't their home, and they wished they
could go back to their friends and families.

Day after day "friends from another planet"
would come to the People Zoo and try to feed them
and play with them, but the people just lay there,
wishing that they were back at home.

Some people were born at the People Zoo. They would curiously listen to stories from other people who had lived on the outside of their cages before they were taken away to live at The People Zoo.

They would then imagine what it was like to be free and live in the place that their families once did.

Because the "friends from another planet" had such
big hearts, seeing the people in the People Zoo
sad and upset didn't make them happy.

They decided to return all the people back to
their homes and to their families. They would find a
different way to learn about human people, and a
different way to teach their children about how
people lived, thought, played, and loved.

It was then that the "friends from another planet" realized that the best way to learn about people was to live with them, respect them, and share their happiness, hopes, and dreams, and to open their hearts to them.

Together the people and the "friends from another planet" started living together in peace and harmony and the world became a better place.

THE
END

Meet
Octavia Lindlahr

Octavia Lindlahr is a mother of three children (Seth, Alex, and Max), and grandmother to one (Ollin). She is an avid animal rights activist. She is the owner/founder of "Outside the Box," a Child Development Center for typical and special needs children that has a focus on learning through multi-sensory experience and play, and fosters attachment and bonding. Octavia is also the Founder of a Mindfulness Program for children 4 – 12 years old called F.L.O.W. Her educational background is in Child Development, English Literature, Theology and Neurobiology, however writing has always been a passion of hers. She is currently writing a children's book series about children who have special gifts and talents, as well as working on novel that is a paranormal/love story. Her wish is that as a society, humans learn to value animals and learn to live with them in peace and harmony as Earthlings. Octavia lives in West Hills, California with her husband Markus, youngest son Max, and two beloved dogs, Beau and Lola.

Lightning Source UK Ltd.
Milton Keynes UK
UKHW021017050120
356353UK00004B/15/P